EXPEDITION TO PLUTO

©2020 Positronic Publishing

Hardcover ISBN 13: 978-1-5154-4692-7
Trade Paperback ISBN 13: 978-1-5154-4693-4
E-book ISBN 13: 978-1-5154-4694-1

EXPEDITION TO PLUTO

by Fletcher Pratt and Laurence Manning

Within the Goddard's hurtling hull Captain "Steel-Wall" McCausland, hero of the space fleets, nursed his secret plan for an Earth reborn. Reuter the scientist cuddled his treacherous test-tubes. And Air Mate Longworth grappled an unseen horror that menaced a billion lives!

"Now passing Phobos, the second moon of Mars. From this point to the orbit of Jupiter we are in the planetoid belt, the most dangerous portion of our voyage. This ship's armor of twenty-inch beryll-steel may be perfectly adequate to keep meteorites out, but let just one of those planetoids, little worlds, hit us and this broadcast would end right now. Here we are! Phobos at our left and down, if there is any up or down out here in empty space. It's a little red moon, cracked and seamed, all rock; it has no atmosphere and no weather. The rocks stand up, jagged and sharp. There she goes! Good-bye Phobos—we're making 9,250 miles an hour past Phobos, according to a message from Captain McCausland which has just been handed to me. The Captain doesn't look well this morning. He seems depressed and the difficulties of this expedition are weighing on him. That's all for today. This is 7-LOP, the interplanetary expedition ship *Goddard*, on the exploring expedition to Pluto. Your reporter, Paulette de Vries speaking. Interplanetary time 0-six-0-0, May 24, 2432."

The girl snapped the key of her microphone off and turned angrily to the young man who had tapped her on the shoulder. "What do you mean by interrupting my broadcast, Adam Longworth?"

The tall young man was frowning at her. "You know the crew listens in on these broadcasts, don't you?"

"Well, what am I supposed to do about that? Give three cheers?"

"Listen, Paulette. On an expedition as dangerous as this, is it right to let the crew know the Captain is feeling depressed or doubtful? I didn't mean to make you sign off, though."

"I signed off because I was through. Don't flatter yourself! Trouble with you is you try to run everybody's business. I thought you might have got over that in the ten years since I knew you in school, but you haven't. Trying to keep me out of the control room so I wouldn't hurt myself! Wake up, Mr. Longworth, this is 2432; you're still living back in the nineteen-hundreds

5

when woman's place was in the home."

Longworth glanced at a bandage around the girl's left wrist. Paulette reddened.

"All right, I slipped and sprained my wrist. So what? So you have my things moved to another cabin, where I'll be more comfortable. You're an interfering old woman, Mr. Longworth. You're hopeless!"

Longworth reddened uncomfortably.

"Very well, Paulette, I'll stop interfering as you call it. But really, you ought to stop referring to the Captain in such a manner as to break down the morale of the expedition."

The girl glared at him. "I'll take orders about that kind of thing from Captain McCausland and nobody else. And I don't think the man I'm going to marry will censor what I have to say."

Adam Longworth's face set as he stood for a moment irresolute. Then, as Paulette said nothing more, he turned and left the cabin. Outside he paused, gazing down the long main corridor of the space ship toward the open fo'castle lock, where the crew lolled in the month-long idleness of space-voyaging. He frowned, strode off to find Captain McCausland.

*

Captain McCausland—"Old Steel-Wall" as he was known in the League of Planets Space Service—was poring over the course plotted on the chart table. The handsome, saturnine face and straight back were those of a youth; but he was forty-five and had twenty years of service behind him and had won the honor medals of three planets. He was so absorbed that he did not notice the Mate till Longworth touched his arm.

"Yes?" he said, turning round with a pair of dividers in his hand.

"It can wait sir, if you're busy."

McCausland looked at him out of cold, efficient eyes. "Speak up."

"It's the crew, sir. You know how these long runs are. Months with nothing to do, nothing to see."

There was a flicker around the Captain's mouth that might have been amusement. "Trouble?"

Adam looked startled. "Oh, no, nothing yet. I just wanted to head off trouble before it started, sir. You heard Miss de Vries broadcast just now?"

Captain McCausland nodded, and this time the smile of amusement was definitely present. "I think the word was 'depressed' wasn't it? And you're afraid it will throw the crew into a panic, and they'll turn the ship around on us and head for home. Is that it, Mr. Longworth?"

Adam, wishing he were anywhere but just there, and wilting visibly under the sarcastic gaze of the Captain, plunged desperately ahead. "Well, sir, I took the liberty of asking her not to do it again.... She said she was taking orders only from you ... that is ... I'm sorry, sir, I didn't know you were going to...."

"To be married, you mean? Well, why not?" He smiled again. "The ceremony will take place as soon as we come back from this expedition. That gives her a certain amount of privilege you understand." His face turned suddenly grave and his voice a trifle sharp. "Moreover, Miss de Vries is here as radio reporter for the Interplanetary broadcasting. I want you to understand, Mr. Mate, that I'll have no interference with her. Instead of chasing bugaboos, suppose you check the course through the planetoid belt. I'll leave you with it; that will give you something real to worry about for a change."

Adam stared hopelessly after his retreating back. Damnation! Everything had seemed to go wrong since the beginning of this voyage. The harder he tried to prove himself worthy of the appointment as second-in-command to "Old Steel-Wall" the worse things went. With a shrug he turned doggedly to the chart work.

Two hours later he stepped over to the chart-room port and gazed out into the velvet blue-black of space where the thousand suns of the Milky Way burned across the horizon. It was no use. He was going to have to make a fool of himself again.

But could he help it? Captain McCausland had certainly asked him to check the course through the planetoid belt. Perhaps he would forget now, and not ask about the checking operation. But if he did? Certainly Walter McCausland couldn't have been wrong. Yet the figures—? Adam studied his work sheet again, shaking his head.

"Finished the checking, Longworth?" The voice startled him so that he jumped.

"Yes, sir. Shall I take over the watch, sir?"

"Little early, aren't you? What do you think of the course, Mister?"

Adam hesitated.

"It seems ... likely to get us there, sir."

McCausland's eyes became points. "Are you by any chance evading my question? I'll repeat it. It was—what do you think of the course? What is your opinion?"

Adam gulped. Here it was.

"There seems to be a fault in it, sir. I'm sorry."

"Indeed?" The tone was sarcastic. "Elucidate, Mister Mate."

"It takes us up out of the plane of the ecliptic, then back again beyond the planetoid belt. That's very good, sir, and quite safe, but didn't you omit the fuel consumption factor? The course as plotted gives two shifts of forty-five degrees each, or half a complete stop, as far as fuel is concerned. It would cut down the amount of fuel available for exploration on Pluto to—well, here are the figures as I've worked them out. We'd have about enough for two or three landings. But if we went right through the danger belt of the planetoids as originally planned, we would save enough fuel to really explore the planet. We have to explore thoroughly if we're going to find beryllium there. It won't lie on the surface. Why, it's hardly worth going on at all if we can't do any more exploring than that.... That's my opinion, sir, and I didn't volunteer it, and I ask your pardon in advance."

*

The great space captain smiled easily. "No need to beg my pardon at all. At first glance one would think you had the right of it, but I just happen to have gone into the matter a little deeper. You understand the reasons behind this voyage? Well, suppose that after having been away for two years we come back right on schedule, but without a load of beryllium, without having found any trace of it. What will happen? The League of Planets simply orders out another expedition, better equipped, and we go down as having failed."

"But Captain! In two years there may not be enough light alloys left on the three planets to build another ship as big as this! The service to Mars will have to be stopped long before that. The lithium mines there can't operate unless the water supply from Venus is maintained."

"Well, what of it? Nobody likes to work in that Martian colony."

Adam caught his breath.

"But how are the atomic motors that do all the work going to operate without the lithium from Mars?"

"And what of that, even? It would be temporary. Just a few months or years till another expedition could be sent out. You take things too seriously. What is there to prove that some other method of armoring space-ships won't be found? Beryllium may not be necessary after all."

"Perhaps you're right." Adam was still skeptical. "But is it likely, sir? You've been on the space run so long you haven't kept up with chemistry. The armor against meteorites now is so thick that any metal but beryllium would double the weight of the vessel, and even with these seven million horsepower Buvier-Manleys we couldn't make the run from Venus to Mars. Why, sir, it would mean the end of the lithium mines, it would mean the end of atomic power, and we'd have to go back to the barbarism of the twentieth century, when they ran everything by electricity from waterfalls!"

Captain McCausland raised an athletic hand. "Spare me that, Mister Mate! I have heard it at approximately a hundred banquets before starting out on this expedition. Yes, we carry the fate of the world and all that. We have to find beryllium or else the Mars mines can't be run and the atomic motors stop. I could sing it in my sleep. But suppose we do take chances and get this ship wrecked. Won't the world have to go back to 'barbarous' electric power after all? For my part, I think some of those people in the twentieth century probably had a good time."

Adam was silent. There was something in the Captain's reasoning, he felt. Yet he, Adam Longworth, could not but feel that the issue was a desperately serious one for every inhabitant of the three worlds—Earth, Venus and Mars—belonging to the planetary league. The entire known supply of beryllium, the precious light, strong metal that was alone suitable for the armor of space ships, had been exhausted. All that remained was in the hulls of the few dozen ships carrying water from Venus to Mars, and from the arid deserts of Mars, bringing to Earth the equally precious lithium which was the only material with which atomic motors could be powered.

Every year, in spite of the best of care, one or two space ships would be wrecked—caught in the sun's gravitational field, or lost through some small error of navigation. Soon there would be no more space ships; and no more could be built. Each of the outer planets had been explored in turn—each but the last, the outermost and most distant; Pluto. They were on their way there now; if they could not make it—

"Very well, sir," he said aloud. "I see your point. Will you take over the controls at the change of course?"

"I'll take over now. Report in two hours.... One more thing, Longworth. You're young, damn young, to be first mate on this expedition. You know you were a last-minute choice, because of an accident to a much more experienced, and from what I've seen so far, a much better man. Make the most of your chance, but don't forget I'm captain here. I can't go into my reasons for everything I do. That's all, Mister Mate."

*

"Hello, Earth! This is Paulette de Vries speaking, aboard 7-LOP, space-ship Goddard . For the last two days we have been running along the first leg of the angle that will lift us over the dangerous belt of tiny planets thirty million miles beyond Mars. In a few minutes, the ship's motors will be started to turn our course again—straight for Pluto. I'm going to turn you over to the microphone in the motor compartment and let you listen as the seven-million-horse-power atomics take hold. Jake Burchall is in charge down there at the motors.... Ready, Jake? Take it away!

... "That's all, folks. We're on the new course, with the engines shut off, and we'll coast along for eight months at a speed of two miles a second, 120 miles a minute, 7,200 miles an hour toward Pluto. Nothing for anyone to do—a nice vacation for eight months. *We're giving a costume ball, folks; it's all we can think of. It won't be much of a ball, though, as I'm the only woman aboard. I'm going to lend some of the space-men some of my dresses—"* (CRASH!)

"What was that, quick—!"

She got the answer, and went on.

"*It's all right, just one of the incidents of interplanetary navigation. Hit by a meteorite. Out here above the planetoid zone and close to Jupiter meteorites are more common. Here's Mr. Wayland, one of the junior officers, with a report. What's the damage, Mr. Wayland? It is! Folks back on Earth, we surely got it that time! The meteorite penetrated! Right through the twenty-inch beryll-steel armor of our hull into compartment eighteen. The whole wall of the hull is crushed in there, we've lost a few hundred cubic feet of air, but the doors are closed and our air supply is safe. Here's First Mate Longworth, just back from compartment eighteen. He says they'll leave the compartment as it is, and build a tunnel of thin metal through it to reach the five compartments toward the stern.*

"*Folks, can you imagine the shock of that meteorite? It's only a foot through and weighs five hundred pounds. If it had been one of the planetoids our whole hull would be crushed now. Captain McCausland turned our course to avoid the planetoid zone entirely and does that prove he was right? It does, and how! Well, folks, it's been a long day and an exciting one. This is 7-LOP, space-ship* Goddard *, signing off. Paulette de Vries speaking. O-nine-two-seven, May 27, 2432.*"

*

Adam had returned from the damaged compartment in time to catch the close of the broadcast as he was stripping off the space suit in which he was making the examination. Dog-tired, he had just switched off the light preparatory to turning in when the light and buzzer flashed at the door.

"It's me, Jake," came a voice.

The First Mate switched on the light, and called: "Come in."

A small man, his face seamed by a thousand wrinkles, slipped through the door almost furtively and stood, twisting his hands in the audition helmet which enabled him to hear in the engine room above the noise of the motors.

"Didn't think you'd be in bed so soon, Mr. Adam," he apologized. "But you always was an early retirer. I remember when I had you on the training ship—he—he—he." He ended on a kind of nervous little giggle, and Adam looked at him sharply.

"Yes, I remember. I couldn't cork off for a minute without hearing someone pounding on the door and you yelling, 'It's Jake Burchall! Time to get up'" His face sobered. "You didn't come here to talk about old times, Jake. What's on your mind?"

"Well, you know how one thing and another gets around on a long run like this. I didn't know but maybe there was something I could help you about, sort of, he—he—he."

"Afraid not, Jake. Everything on hand is up to me. You can tell me one thing, though. I was just in from the Mars run when I found my name posted for this expedition, and I never did hear whose place I got as First Mate on this trip. Do you know who it was?"

"Didn't nobody tell you that? It was Blagovitch."

"Why, he's one of the most cautious men in the service! What happened to him?"

"Bruk his foot. He-he-he. There was some said he did it on purpose."

"But what could Old Steel-Wall—that is, why did the Captain pick him in the first place?"

"Well, Mr. Adam, there's a lot of things about this trip ain't the same as an ordinary run. I wonder myself sometimes. The Cap'n, he picks a course way out of the ecliptic to dodge planetoids he didn't stand one chance in a million of hitting anyhow; and he picks him a mighty cautious mate, and then he picks him a young mate when the other one can't go. What's he 'fraid of?"

"He's afraid of failing, that's all, Jake."

"He-he-he. Well, maybe I'm a old fool. I'd say it was more like he was 'fraid of succeeding."

*

MANNING AND PRATT

"Hello, Earth! This is your radio gal, Paulette de Vries, speaking from 7-LOP, space-ship Goddard. *Interplanetary time two-two-0-three, or just three seconds behind schedule for entering the atmosphere of Pluto. We're falling rapidly toward the planet. I can only see half of it, filling the entire horizon. The color is almost exactly that of a pearl in moonlight, white with blue lights and absolutely featureless. Sunlight out here is indescribably weak. Our spectroscope, handled by Professor Reuter, shows the atmosphere is high in fluorine, with traces of argon, and outside that a thin belt, a very thin belt of helium and hydrogen. I told you all that the other day. We have accurate temperature readings now, folks, and what they say is 200 degrees below zero, which is plenty chilly. You could drive a nail with a butter hammer at that temperature, folks, and it means we will have to do our exploring by diving, since the whole surface of the planet will be covered, perhaps miles deep, by liquid gases. Can't tell till we get there. Once we do get in, however, these talks will temporarily cease, folks. I'll be sorry, because I've enjoyed them, and I've enjoyed hearing from all of you back on Earth, so many million miles away. But I'll be back, and so will all the crew and its heroic captain. You may remember—Stand by! We're in the hydrogen layer now. It's misty, streaming past the ports, so I can hardly see anything. I must sign off now. This is 7-LOP, space-ship* Goddard."

Adam Longworth crouched motionless. The muscles bulged along his arms, shoulder and neck quivered with tension, and perspiration stood in tickling beads on his skin. His eyes were fixed on the control panel before him; on either side was a quartermaster at a set of controls and behind the three stood Captain McCausland, calm and watchful.

Adam's hand moved rapidly and a quivering needle stood still on a dial.

"Three gravities insufficient."

The Captain's finger found a red button on the portable signal panel that made a three-inch medallion on the left breast of his uniform. Throughout the ship there was a flash of red lights; loudspeakers echoed his "Stand by for five gravities."

*

The quartermasters flung long levers; the motors boomed, braking the speed of the *Goddard's* fall toward the surface. Captain McCausland slumped

13

to the acceleration and recovered; the air-speed indicator crept toward the bottom of the dial, and had almost reached it, when a loudspeaker twanged nasally. "Visibility fifty feet, liquid surface. Forty feet—going down—afloat, sir."

Adam killed the motor with a plunge of his finger and his ears rang in the sudden stillness.

"Thank you, gentlemen," said the Captain. "Perfect landing, Mister Longworth. Relieve the navigation watch and report to the chart-room in ten minutes."

Adam saluted, said a few words to the quartermasters and went out with them to the fo'castle. The men off watch were just unstrapping themselves from their bunks. Jake Burchall stepped up.

"Do I take up the new watch, Mr. Adam?"

"Two hours from now. Look here, Jake, there's something I wish you'd do."

"Yes sir."

Adam lowered his voice.

"Did you hear the report? Fluorine all through this planet. Our ports are glass, and fluorine acts on glass. They're thick, of course, and have layers of plastic, but it will wear them through eventually. We've got to think of something to do about it, and I think I have the answer. Remember compartment eighteen? She'll be flooded. Suppose when you're posting that watch you get into a space suit and slide in there. Don't go outside, but cut loose some of the mica lining around the break. When you get it, you can make some mica sheets for the helmet view-ports of your space suit. Then get into compartment eighteen again, and try it out. I'm no chemical expert, but mica should insulate the view-ports on the helmet, and if it'll do that, it will insulate the view-ports of the whole ship. Report to me privately. I don't want to make a fool of myself if Professor Reuter already has some other scheme worked out."

Jake grinned in understanding.

"Yes sir. He-he-he. Hope he hasn't."

In the chart room, when Adam arrived, he found a small gathering.

Perkins, the chemists, was there; so was Professor Reuter, the astronomical man, a couple of assistants, and Captain McCausland, looking extremely grave, thoughtful, but ruffled.

"Well, Longworth," he said. "You're just in time to order out the navigation watch and set the course back to Earth."

Adam was aghast. "Not really?"

"Ask these gentlemen." He indicated the scientists.

Professor Reuter cleared his throat, but it was Perkins who spoke. "At least we cannot remain here. The fluorine here will gradually, but certainly, cut through the glass in this ship."

*

Adam flushed. He burst out: "But you knew there was fluorine a month ago! Didn't anyone—?"

Captain McCausland raised his hand. "Please."

Professor Reuter explained. "To tell the truth there was some discussion at that time. I am afraid I must confess myself considerably at fault. Dr. Perkins at that time urged that the expedition return and install quartz ports on the *Goddard*. At that time I judged the temperature would be about what it is, minus 200, and at that figure fluorine would not be present in the liquid portion of the atmosphere, but would exist as a gas, and therefore would not make contact with our ports while diving."

"I warned you it would be in solution," remarked Dr. Perkins.

"Yes." Professor Reuter, a big man, with folds of fat hanging from his cheeks, pursed his lips and blew through them. "At the time, I must confess, I really must confess, that I failed to consider the fact that the enveloping upper atmosphere of the planet would cause the surface temperature to be lower than that in the atmosphere itself. As a result, it is just cold enough to hold a certain amount of fluorine in solution in this cold ocean—"

"And, in a nut-shell, we must turn back," said Adam. He appealed to Captain McCausland. "Isn't there anything aboard ship with which we could insulate the ports?" Scientists always made difficulties, he thought; an old space captain like McCausland would not be so hard to down.

"We can try putting divers in space suits with double-thickness glass in the ports. That would last a couple of hours at all events. I don't doubt but we could get volunteers in *this* crew."

Reuter blew through his thick lips again. "Dangerous. As scientific head of the expedition I will permit nothing of the kind. Naturally, Captain, we are under your orders, but if you take such a step it will be without my authority."

McCausland made a gesture of hopelessness. "Have you any other ideas to suggest, Mister Longworth?"

Was "Old Steel-Wall" giving up this easily? Adam's thoughts wheeled, but he schooled himself to inquire mildly, "Have you thought of trying mica windows, sir?"

"That would do it!" cried Dr. Perkins excitedly. "Fluorine doesn't attack mica—at least at Earth temperatures. I don't know about these sub-zero atmospheres, but it ought to work. Have we the mica?"

"The ship is lined with it," remarked McCausland. "But we can't very well take the ship apart."

"Compartment eighteen, sir!" Adam burst out.

"Try it by all means: Hurry though, for we'll have to shutter the ship's ports within an hour or get out of here. I congratulate you, Mister Longworth. That was well thought of."

Was there a touch of irony in the voice? As Adam saluted and withdrew, he wondered. Nobody else appeared to have noticed it, to have noticed that there was something in the Captain's voice that didn't somehow sound quite right.

*

Three men were grouped around the air lock at eighteen, and they looked up as the First Mate approached. "He's coming out now, sir," said one of them. "Been in already once, and Bjornsen fitted a mica shield over one of his helmet ports. He's trying that and the straight glass shield in comparison."

Adam nodded wordlessly, watching the lock handle. Presently it turned and out stumbled a figure like a gnome, cased in hairy hoar-frost. "Pretty cold out there," said one of the men, as with gloved fingers he labored deftly at Burchall's helmet.

The little wizened face came out of it, grinning like a monkey's. "It works, sir! I was in a good five minutes. Look here—the glass lens is all pitted and scored, but the mica isn't touched. Something funny out there in that ocean, though."

"What do you mean?"

"Something with legs, only they weren't exactly legs, either—"

"Careful with that space suit there, Jake. Material's brittle after that cold."

Adam raised his voice. "Look here men. We have a job on our hands. We must make and install port covers for every port on the ship. You know, the regular collision covers—beryll-steel. Jake, go up forward and get a dozen men, while you, Bjornsen, fix those mica covers on a dozen space suit helmets. Make it snappy, for Heaven's sake. We have just one hour to work in."

"Beg pardon, sir, but wouldn't it be easier to do it outside this atmosphere?"

"Haven't the fuel. Hurry!"

The ship rang with orderly disorder, as man after man of the off-duty watch reported, received the space suit with the new mica windows, and passed out through the air-lock in compartment eighteen to join the others who were adjusting protective collision-shutters over the big ship's ports. The last man through, Adam embarked on an inspection tour of the ship. Compartment 23 checked—all ports shuttered; compartment 22—

A bell rang violently, and the loudspeaker system shouted: "First Mate Longworth wanted in the Captain's cabin at once. First Mate Longworth wanted—"

"First Mate Longworth reporting," Adam remarked into his chest phone, and hurried along the corridor.

Captain McCausland was seated at his desk, drumming on it with his fingers. "Mister Mate," he burst out, as Adam entered, "do you know what time it is?"

"No, sir."

The Captain indicated the space-chronometer set in the wall. "Your hour is up. Call your men in. We're leaving."

"But, sir, they're nearly finished—"

"Mister Mate, I have taken the trouble to explain my orders to you once before. I'll do it once more, so there will be no possible mistake. I'm responsible for the safety of this expedition and the lives of the people aboard. In the present case it's my responsibility to see that this cold fluorine ocean doesn't eat through the ports and put everyone to a horrible death, corroding as it freezes them—including Miss de Vries. Call in your men. That's an order!"

Adam's mind filled suddenly with the picture of Paulette struggling vainly to beat back the hideous icy wave of acid at a temperature lower than anything on Earth, of.... He lifted his chest phone and spoke slowly. "Working party outside; abandon work and return at once. Enter by lock in compartment eighteen."

*

The sound of hammers and the grind of wrenches on the outer hull went on uninterrupted. An expression of surprise spread across Adam's face; Captain McCausland's darkened with anger. "First Mate Longworth speaking! Did you hear me? Burchall, answer at once!"

Again that pause, punctuated only by the sound of tools. McCausland lifted his own phone. "Burchall! Heinstatt! Captain McCausland speaking! Answer at once." Again no reply but the mocking tap of hammers. The Captain's face flushed darkly.

"Longworth, if this is more of your officiousness, I'll have your badges! Mister Longworth, you will get into a space suit at once and bring those men in. Knock them out if necessary."

Adam ran down the corridor toward the compartment eighteen air lock thinking to himself that if this was a mutiny it came at the most fortunate time for the success of the expedition. He took his time donning the space suit, his time about entering the air lock and turning on the pressure jets that would clear the way before him into the icy ocean outside. Just as he was about to throw open the outer door of the lock, the indicator on it moved, it was flung open from the outside, and the first of the divers stumbled in, accompanied by a rush of the icy sea that began immediately to vaporize in the warmer space of the compartment. The clang of hammers outside sank to a tap, then ceased altogether. The work was done! They could float on that Plutonian sea for as long as necessary without danger.

When they were out of compartment eighteen's air lock again, with the helmets off, Adam turned to Jake Burchall.

"Why didn't you answer me or Captain McCausland just now? Didn't you know you could be sent to the mines on Mars for disobedience?"

"Didn't hear you, sir. You see, we was in such a hurry to get out that we kind of forgot to put our radiophones on the helmets."

Before Adam could put another question the bell clamored for lunch.

*

Aboard the space-ship *Goddard* the fiction of keeping up the normal twenty-four-hour Earth day was maintained, and it was not till after the meal called, by courtesy, lunch that Adam again faced Captain McCausland across the desk of his cabin. Paulette de Vries was on the Captain's other side as Adam entered and saluted stiffly.

"Your report, Mister Mate? I am anxious to learn why my orders weren't obeyed."

"No radiophones on the suits, sir."

The Captain stared, taken aback. At last he nodded his acceptance of the wholly reasonable explanation.

"Very well.... Glad you got the shutters installed in time. As matters stand, then, we can remain here for some time. Professor Reuter reports we are near one of the poles of this planet. We might as well start exploring here as anywhere. Will you take the detail?"

Adam's face lighted. He hadn't expected a chance like this. "I'd be delighted, sir," he began, and then, catching sight of Paulette's slightly disdainful smile, broke off short.

"Very good. Take at least one good man with you. Professor Reuter says the depth here is about sixty feet, which is the equivalent of thirty feet on Earth, due to the difference in gravity. That is, the pressure ought not to bother anyone in a space suit provided the depth is constant. I'm sending you because you made good on that mica stunt. Now here's your chance to do something bigger. You'll have complete charge of whatever party you take."

"Mr. Longworth will enjoy that very much," remarked Paulette. "He likes to take complete charge of things."

"I've noticed that," said McCausland, drawing down the corner of his mouth. He reached into a drawer, and producing one of the ugly, ungainly rocket-pistols, shoved it across the desk. "This thing fires the new atomic shells. Pretty dangerous, as you probably know, but it's about the only thing that will work in these liquid densities, and you can't tell what you'll run into out there. Good luck!"

Adam saluted, and was just turning away when out of the corner of his eye he caught sight of Paulette's face. It had gone suddenly rather white, and her lips were slightly parted. He turned back to speak, but the moment had passed, and contenting himself with an awkward repetition of the salute he made his way out of the cabin.

*

Jake Burchall, responding to a call over the loud speaker system, found him changing into the electrically warmed clothes used in the depths of outer space.

"Want to come with me, Jake? An hour or so scouting along the ocean floor. We'll be the first men to land on Pluto."

To his surprise, the wizened little man, instead of bursting into his habitual giggle, looked thoughtful.

"What's the matter, Jake?"

"Nothin', Mr. Adam. I was just wonderin', that's all, if maybe you volunteered for this, but I don't s'pose you'd care to tell."

"I don't mind telling you. Captain McCausland assigned me."

Burchall scratched his head, evidently seeking to choose his words.

"You think a mighty lot of him, don't you, Mr. Adam?"

Adam stopped dressing with a zipper half closed, his mouth open. "Why sure! Ever since I was a kid—I remember being brought up on the story of how Steel-Wall McCausland saved the Venus mail rocket, the time—"

"Yes, I know, Mr. Adam. But looky here, I'm goin' to tell you for your own good, there some folks think Old Steel-Wall is a little bit too smooth outside and too hard inside, and I ain't satisfied. There's some mighty funny things goin' on. I don't like the way he called us in from that port detail—and that there navigation around the planetoids—and this here exploring trip—I'm just maybe a old fool, but I got my ideas."

"Bunk, Jake. Captain McCausland has other people to think of, too...." Adam's sentence trailed off as he remembered the Captain's willingness to give up the expedition when they had landed on the wet surface of Pluto. Could it be possible that the hero of his boyhood, the man Paulette was going to marry—?

"What have you got there?" Jake Burchall's voice interrupted his chain of thought. "I s'pose the Captain gave you that, too?" inquired the old engineer, picking up the rocket pistol, and when Adam nodded. "Not for mine, Mr. Adam. Them things is twict as dangerous to you as to whatever you shoot 'em at. Come back there with me to the engine room. I got some of those marble bombs stuck on long rods back there. When you poke something with them, you know the explosion isn't going to blow you into the middle of next week."

Cased like lobsters in their space suits the pair waddled clumsily up the spiral ramp to the main outlet lock. The pair of duty men at the lock swung the handles in a bored manner, and just as he was entering Adam thought he caught another glimpse of Paulette around the corner of the corridor, and raised one sheathed arm to wave her farewell, but she did not answer.

"All right, Jake?" called Adam through the chest phone. There was a series of clicks. "All right, Mr. Adam."

Adam swung the lock control and felt the grip of the pale ocean, colder than anything on , sliding up around his legs, to his waist. Another spin of the handle, and side by side the two were settling gently through the opalescent depths toward the surface of Pluto.

*

Inside the ship, the lock attendants had gone off duty and the corridor was for the moment empty. Paulette glanced at the pressure gauge, saw that it registered a blank, which meant that the two had left the lock, and then turned swiftly to look along the corridor. No one in sight.

"At least," Walter had said to her, "wait till those two come back. You don't know what may be in that ocean out there—an ocean of liquid air and fluorine. Dr. Perkins says we don't know a thing about the climates of these extreme cold planets, and what forms of life may exist. Think of those horrible quick-acting fungi that destroyed the explorers of the first Uranus expedition."

"But you practically ordered Mate Longworth to go," she had retorted.

"That's different. Danger is his business."

There was no point in arguing. She left it at that, and promising Walter to rejoin him later, strolled down the corridor and up the ramp to the outer airlock. But danger was her business, too, she told herself, as she swung back the door to the compartment in which the space suits were kept, and hastily took down the smallest on the rack. Yes, the eye-pieces were mica-covered.

Danger was her business, she told herself again, as she turned on the pressure jets to clear the lock; she was Paulette de Vries, the radio gal, chosen for her part in this expedition out of all the radio recorders of three planets for her utter fearlessness. And besides, that snip of a First Mate, Adam Longworth, had intimated that she needed protection. The lock snapped to behind her, and as it did so, she thought exultantly that Captain Walter McCausland might as well learn now as any other time that he couldn't order his prospective wife around, even if he could make everyone else aboard the *Goddard* jump.

*

The water was very dark, the color of bottle glass, splotched here and there with darker, purplish shadows. Far above her, Paulette could see the faint shimmering line of light that marked the space ship. It looked to be hundreds of feet above her. Five steps in any direction, she knew, would blot it out completely. She had no great fear of getting lost, as the compass guide at her belt was tuned to the ship's control compass and would always point to it. Somewhere down here in the dark around her Adam and Jake were also exploring the bottom. Although she couldn't see them, the thought gave her courage. She stepped tentatively forward. One—two—three—four—five—at each step floating a little before she came down. She could no longer see the faint, comfortable lights of the ship somewhere above her, and for a brief moment, panic tore at her throat. She fought it down. Silly! She peered around her, as though the thought of Jake and Adam would make them materialize. There! There they were. She could see them dimly, like shadows, to her left. She turned and walked as swiftly as she could in the direction. How Adam would laugh at her for her fears. What a little coward—. She stopped suddenly, and cold, clammy fingers of fear rippled along her spine. The dark shadow before her wasn't Adam or Jake! It was something tall and thin. Something that seemed alive, weaving back and forth, and about the same color as the water. It seemed about ten feet high and six inches through, and was made up of sections like a string of sausages. Then over to the right she saw more of them—a regular forest.

Like the snapping of a brittle icicle, the tension broke. They were plants. Some form of natural flora, swaying to and fro in the icy currents of that dark sea. She laughed hysterically, and relief flooded her, bathing her in perspiration. But the experience had nevertheless unnerved her. Coward or not, she decided she had had enough, and turned to find her way back to the ship. Then she saw it! Behind and a little above her. Something big, whiter than the color of the water, hovering, drifting. She tried to hurry. Tried to tell herself it was just another surprising but inanimate form of life to be found in this strange planet, but as she glanced back and up, she saw the thing was keeping perfect pace with her. Horrified, she watched as it settled slowly toward her. Huge. White. Hideously opaque. She couldn't move. She could only stand, rooted as in some frightful nightmare, staring with bursting

23

eyes as the thing drifted gently toward her. Then panic took her. She opened her mouth to scream, but no sound came from her strangling throat, and her tongue clove tightly to the roof of her mouth. She put her arms up, like a child trying to push aside a horrible dream. Her hands touched a soft, white pulpy body. Touched it, then to her utter horror *passed through into the body itself!* They were gripped in that opaque substance. And still the thing settled lower, like a great hideous, white cloak. It would cover her completely. *Absorb her.* As it had absorbed her hands. As it was even now absorbing her wrists—her arms....

*

Adam and Jake Burchall had set out with the idea of tracing a circle of some 300 yards around the ship. In spite of the weak gravity, the pressure was against them, and at each long, floating step they paused while Adam probed into the silt of the ocean floor with a long rod. Rock surface was only inches down; what kind of rock he could not tell. At each step they encountered the same sausage-like chain-weeds Paulette had met, and twice Adam attempted to pull up one of the singular Plutonian plants, only to find it breaking into sections at a touch.

"I suspect," said Adam through his phone, "that these are some very low form of life. Look how they break along the joint, Jake. They probably reproduce in that fashion, breaking off to form an entirely new plant."

"Funny we haven't seen any other form of life."

"Yes. It would be more usual to find a couple of hundred on an ocean floor like this."

A surge in the water round them nearly swept the explorers from their feet. Adam looked up. Scarcely ten feet above him, a huge brownish globe shot past, twice his own height, its smooth surface studded with countless tiny arms that beat the water in unison. As he gazed at it, a paler, whitish mass soared through the twilight to leap on the brown globe, and twisting in each other's grip, they passed from sight.

Jake's gasp came through the earphones and then his giggle, "He—he—he, Mr. Adam, there's two more forms of life and we make another one, if we

24

stay alive till we get back."

Another three steps, and they halted again at the sight of a shapeless, almost white mass looming through the fog of green ahead. It was alive; it moved, but flowing, rather than swimming, and as nearly as they could make out in the dimness was without eyes, mouth or visible organs of any kind, a huge, shapeless jelly. Adam reached for the rocket pistol at his belt, but Jake's eye had caught the motion and his voice came through the earphones, "Don't use that thing, Mr. Adam. It ain't—Holy catfish!"

The huge colorless jelly had sidled toward them through the water, then sheered off, revealing as it did so, a core of some darker color through its translucent sides and three shapeless legs whose motion propelled it. As it made the turn away from the explorers it bumped one of the curious segmented weeds and Jake had cried out.

*

For where the animal had bumped the weed a huge dent appeared in its rounded forward end, growing rapidly till it was a cavern, a cavern which engulfed the chain-weed. Instantly the lips of the cavern closed; Adam could see that the surface had become as smooth as before, while inside the translucent structure of the animal the outline of the weed was faintly visible.

"I've seen things like that before," said Adam softly, as though fearful of attracting the monster's attention.

"Where? I ain't never seen nothing like that. And I'm telling you, Mr. Adam, I been around a lot. Even in those dinosaur swamps on Venus."

"Ever look through a microscope, Jake?"

"Can't say as I have very often, Mr. Adam."

"That's just what you see in a microscope, Jake. That brown thing was just like a rotifer. Those big white lumps, that can turn themselves into mouths anywhere they want to and then close up and turn themselves into stomachs, they're amoebas. Amoebas as big as whales! They're the most savage animals in the whole created kingdom—and just about the most dangerous for their size."

The engineer's voice was doubtful. "You mean we're sort of in a

25

microscope?"

Adam grunted.

"Microscope my left foot! Those things are real! They're dangerous! They're the lowest form of life, but what happened is probably that they couldn't develop into any higher forms on this cold planet, so they simply grew to gigantic size. Let's get out of here."

He took off in a long soaring step that carried him jerkily six feet through the water, Jake following. They had progressed perhaps three leaps, when the engineer's voice was suddenly loud inside Adam's helmet—"Look! On the left there!"

Adam checked himself in mid-leap and saw a dark figure in the green gloom of the undersea world, with one of the giant amoebas swooping toward it. "A man!" came Jake's voice. "It's attacking one of the crew. Stand still you, we're coming!"

*

There was no answer; the other diver only put up his arms to ward the thing off, and they saw his hands were empty, weaponless. Another leaping step carried them almost within reach of the hideous thing that at the first touch of the other diver's hands had suddenly formed itself into the huge ingestion funnel. Adam swung his arm back to stab the amoeba with his explosive spear, but Jake's voice came through the earphones.

"Too close, Mr. Adam. He's right on top of that man; you'll blow him to pieces. Let me try to attract him away."

Jake was holding out the harmless end of the spear. He prodded the giant amoeba briskly, and he did so, the jelly-like creature again opened a huge funnel and swooped with a speed surprising for so large and formless an object. Jake dodged and flattened to the sea-bottom, shouting "Give it to him!"

Adam jabbed, pressing the button of his spear as he did so. There was a violent shock; Adam himself went down from the impact of the compressed water and as he fell saw the diver they had rescued tumbling also. Above them a cloud of milky silt boiled up, then whipped away in long ribbons as some obscure current of that strange sea caught it. The giant amoeba loomed through the murk, with a great ragged hole in its side—but the hole was closing, healing before their very eyes!

As he tried to rise and draw the rocket-pistol again, Adam's ears caught Jake's growl of fury, and he saw the engineer lunge with another of the bomb-spears. Again there was the violent shock and murky cloud, half clearing to show Adam the strange diver, who took two staggering steps toward him and then collapsed against his supporting arm. At their feet the giant amoeba, lay, a whitish, shapeless mass, injured beyond the power of a second restoration—but no! As he watched, a foot long bud suddenly projected from the side of the mass, swelled, detached itself, and then slithered off into the dimness.

"Holy catfish!" ejaculated Jake. "You can't kill the thing! Who is it you got there?"

"Don't know. Hello there, hello! Doesn't answer."

"Better get him inside. I'll help."

Together they half dragged, half lifted the diver toward the air-lock, leaped, caught it, and in a few minutes more were in. The lights in the corridor were blinding bright; Jake and Adam snatched off their own helmets, and worked feverishly on the gears of the stranger, to reveal the pale, half-unconscious face of Paulette de Vries.

*

She grinned feebly and licked pale lips.

"Hello, Adam! Oh, boy was I glad to see you a few minutes ago! I thought that thing had me. It was like a bad dream."

"Are you all right? How did you get there?"

"I'm all right now, thanks.... I walked." She got up, a tottering step, and slipped out of her space suit. "I don't need help—excuse me, I'm being ungrateful. What was it?"

"Giant amoeba, I think. He might have found that space suit of yours a little hard to digest, but you would have smothered, waiting for him to discover that. What ever persuaded you to go out there without your

27

headphones connected up or any weapons?"

"Adam Longworth, are you going to lecture me again?" she began, then her face broke into a smile. "Oh, I suppose you're right this time, though. The main reason was really to show Walter that I could do my own thinking, to be honest. And—thank you again."

She held out her hand in gratitude. It lay cool in his for a minute, returning the friendly pressure, and then she was gone.

"I think," said Captain McCausland, "that we can evade any more incidents with these animals of yours by having the digging parties work in an air-lock attached to the ship's entry lock. Diving suits won't be necessary in that case."

"Of course, sir, that would be safer. Won't it use up a good deal of fuel to move the ship for each separate dig, though, sir? We're very low on fuel. May I suggest we pump into storage the amount necessary to make the return voyage? Whatever is left over we can use for exploration from a special tank. When that tank's empty, we're through and we have to go."

"Good suggestion. Give orders accordingly, Mister Mate."

"What would you think of sampling parties, sir, say three well-armed men, chipping off the surface rock wherever they can find it?"

"Waste of time. Beryllium will have to be dug for."

"Where shall we dig, sir? Right here? I understand that beryllium would be closer to the surface near the planet's equator—if there is any."

"You understand? What gave you to understand anything of the kind? Are you the geologist? We'll dig right here. Professor Reuter has made a very exhaustive study of the question and he thinks the pole is much the likeliest spot."

Adam stared. "Professor Reuter! I thought he was an astronomer."

"Reuter is an eminent scientist—which is more than you'll ever be, Mister Mate. You have your work to attend to, and if you do it you'll have no time for doing mine or Professor Reuter's. Now detail an engine-room party to pump fuel for the return trip. Allow ten per cent margin for safety.... What are you staring at me like that for? Do you realize you are impudent! Allow ten per cent. Then report to me how much is left for exploration. Next watch, have the mechanics begin work on the digging lock. By the way—may I have my rocket pistol back?"

Adam remembered that he had handed the pistol to Jake Burchall and had seen it disappear in his capacious pocket. At another time he might have said as much; but in his new-born suspicion of the Captain he merely replied:

"Sorry, sir! Must have dropped it in that fight with the giant amoeba—"

He stopped. For just an instant there had flashed across Walter McCausland's face an expression of fierce, snarling hatred. Then a smooth mask seemed to be drawn across it, and the Captain's voice was serene. "Of course. If it turns up, return it to me. That's all."

*

"But Adam! That's absurd. What possible reason could he have for wishing to make the expedition fail?"

Paulette looked anxiously from Jake Burchall's face to Adam's and back as the three sat in the girl's cabin.

"I know," said Adam. "I don't understand myself, Paulette. Why, he's been a hero of mine ever since I was big enough to know what a space ship looked like! But—"

Jake's wrinkled visage contracted in a frown. "I don't know much about the rest, Miss, but I do know I could have navigated through that planetoid belt myself, and I'm only an engineer. But he certainly used up an awful lot of fuel jumping over it."

"Yes," Adam broke in excitedly, "and he knew there was fluorine in the atmosphere here, but he landed right into it without making any preparation to shutter the ports, though he knew very well fluorine eats into glass like water into sugar. Then he wants to turn back. Then he gives us an impossibly short time to shutter the ports and tries to call in the men and leave before they get it finished. I won't mention—"

The girl burst in on him. "Adam, you're frightfully unfair. There's a perfectly sensible explanation of everything you've mentioned." She held out one hand. "Really, you saved my life down there and I don't want you to think I'm ungrateful, but you're letting things get you. You mustn't think you're running the whole expedition."

Adam's face flushed. He swallowed twice as though about to speak, but before he could say anything, Jake Burchall slowly produced from his pocket the rocket-pistol and laid it on the table before the three.

"Look here, Miss," he said. "I don't want to say nothin', but when I got into my own bunk, I took one of the shells out of this thing. The others are in the magazine. Now I want you to look at this."

He snapped back the catch at the side of the pistol, and two atomic-power shells dropped out—the most powerful and terrible weapons yet invented by the scientists of three planets, ugly little things in their gleaming metal cases. Jake picked up one of them and handed it to Paulette, indicating a spot on the side of the shell with his finger-tip. The girl bent and gazed; there was a tiny pin-prick, a puncture entering the side of the shell.

"Do you see that little hole there?" said Jake. "Do you know what would happen when the trigger was pulled with that shell in the gun? Instead of firing the bullet toward the giant amoeba that hole means the whole force of the charge would have gone off in the gun itself. And that's the gun Captain McCausland gave Adam.... I'm sorry, Miss, I didn't mean to—hurt your feelings."

Paulette had collapsed suddenly across the table, her shoulders shaking with sobs, her face buried in her hands. "Go away, please go away," she cried, as Adam touched her shoulder.

*

"Hello, Earth! This is Paulette deVries reporting progress aboard the Goddard by recording for later broadcast. The first dig ended in a failure this morning. Fifty feet down, and Dr. Perkins reports the composition of the rock strata remarkably uniform in character, but no sign of beryllium in them, nor any formation that looks as though it might contain beryllium. We're on our way from the North Pole of Pluto to the South Pole, where Professor Reuter thinks we stand the best chance of finding the metal we need. Just reached the half way mark.... Hello, the motors have stopped! I'll find out what the reason is for you in just a minute. What's going on, Rossiter?..."

Hello, Earth! Our motors have stopped, the fuel in the special tank we had set aside far exploration purposes is exhausted. We seem to be somewhere near the equator of Pluto.... No, the fuel didn't run out, they've found a leak, a leak in the fuel tank. It's all right, folks, we've set aside enough fuel to ride home to Earth on, but we'll have to dig here instead of at the South Pole. I'm going to ask—"

"Isn't it a curious coincidence, Mister Mate, that this leak should bring us down over the equator—just where you wanted to dig all along?" Captain McCausland's voice was biting.

"Yes, sir."

"Curious coincidence, too, wasn't it, that when those shutters were being put on the workmen's radiophones went out of order? Listen here, Mr. Mate, there have been too damned many coincidences around here to suit me. A few more and you're going to find yourself working in the engine room. That's all. Get out of here and get the digging lock rigged."

Adam saluted mechanically and left the cabin. He knew with sickening precision what the captain meant. Demotion to the engine room would mark him forever in the space service as an inefficient mate. He could never hope to obtain a command of his own, and throughout the rest of his life, wherever he went the record of it would follow him. Even now, the unfavorable report McCausland was sure to turn in when they returned to Earth would block his way to any higher command, any other rating. He felt sick at heart as he joined the group at the main lock, helmet in hand, as they were about to launch themselves into the green ocean below—six men, armed with the bomb-spears Jake Burchall had provided.

He was surprised to note that Paulette deVries was standing waiting with the others, helmet in hand and her face deathly pale.

"Paulette," he begged, "do you really think you should go? Remember what happened last time. Does McCausland—"

"He knows I'm going."

"All right. But keep with the men please. For my peace of mind if not for your own sake. All ready? Close lock!"

The green waters rose about them in the lock and they swung off. Adam's voice came clearly through the earphones of the party.

"Be careful everyone! This is a regular jungle of those chain-weeds."

Paulette's voice answered. "Look, Adam! Where I'm pointing. There's something different over there, little round things, dark red, with a few yellow ones."

"I see them, Paulette. I don't think.... Jake, I don't like this. Let's test that bottom and get back as soon as we can."

The men stooped and scraped in the silt with their metal tools, reporting results. "Not over six inches to rock here." "Eight inches here." "Just about as shallow here as before."

"Take a few samples, then. Make it as quick as you can. As soon as you get your samples move back, be ready to ascend to the main lock."

*

Adam could see nothing but the cloudy liquid around him, stirred to green milk as the sampling of the silt raised a murk around him. "Paulette," he called, "what's your compass reading?"

"Nineteen-O-thirty south. Sixty-three—seven, west."

"I can't see you. Move due east two long steps and stand still. I'll reach for you."

She complied and called out to him.

"What's your reading now?" he asked, and she thought his voice sounded strange as she replied, "Same south reading. Sixty-three—six, west."

"Jake! Where are you and what's your reading?"

"I'm right here, Mr. Adam. Can't see you? This silt doesn't seem to settle down. There's a current of some kind carrying it; I can just stand against it. My reading's eighteen-forty—forty-two south; sixty-two—fifteen west."

"Bjornsen, Rossiter! Report and extend hands. If you don't touch anyone, reach out with the safe ends of your bomb-spears and swing them in a circle till you do.... Ah, who's that who just touched me?"

"Rossiter, sir."

"That makes three of—"

The words were suddenly cut off by the shock of an explosion that nearly tore them from their feet and a heavier cloud of the milky silt came eddying past, fragments of chain-weed moving through it. Burchall's voice came through the earphones. "Attacked! New kind of animal! Eighteen-forty—twenty-one south. Twenty—thirty-two west!"

"Never mind the bearings!" cried Adam. "Rossiter, Paulette! Hang on to the ends of these spears, and take three steps with me, don't lose contact!"

The three leaped as one, then again and again, through the murk in which everything was invisible. As they touched bottom at the end of the last leap, Adam saw a long writhing arm, with a barbed tip at the end of it, swing past his helmet view-ports, caught a gasp from Jake through his earphones, and then felt Paulette at his side pull free from his gripping hand and reach up with the bomb-spear.

There was the shock of another explosion. Down he went, and saw something murky with whirling arms fly past the view-ports. Then Paulette's voice came through, clear and triumphant.

"I got rid of it, Adam, and here's Jake. He's all right, I guess."

"Everyone attention," said Adam, picking himself up. "Make toward the direction where that explosion came from. Then join hands and get back into the ship, quick!"

A few moments later, when the space suits had been put away, and the men were dispersing along the corridors to their cabins, Paulette touched Adam's arm.

"What was the idea of keeping asking for those compass bearings?" she said. "We found the main lock all right, didn't we?"

"Yes," replied Adam shortly, "thanks to your compass. And thanks to you, too, Jake's life was saved. But didn't you hear the reports from those others? Every one of those compasses was wrong, sometimes wrong by a whole degree, and every one was different."

"I don't understand," replied the girl. "Didn't you have the compasses checked before you started?"

"That's just the point. I did have them checked and adjusted. And Professor Reuter was the man who adjusted them. If you hadn't been with us—"

*

"*Hello, Earth! This is Paulette de Vries, speaking to you from Pluto. In about an hour or more we'll be through, one way or another. The digging has gone down to a depth of fifty feet, sheathed in its steel casing, and there's no sign of beryllium yet. We haven't enough fuel to try another dig. I've just been down in the well the men have sunk, looking it over. They're working at the bottom with the new atomic power diggers, that compress the material taken out of the well into a fused, rocklike substance with which the walls of the well itself are lined as they go down, making it safer the deeper they get. One strange thing about the digging so far is that the temperature has advanced sharply as we go down. The ocean from which we're working is two hundred below zero as you know. Down there they struck rock colder than any ice on Earth at the start and had to work in warm air supplied from the ship. Now the temperature has gone up at least a hundred degrees, and it's rising faster with every foot. Just a minute. People are hurrying past me, there's been some kind of an accident at the dig. I'll have the details for you....*"

The girl snapped off her key and hurried down the corridor to the open lock. Above her the loudspeaker system was booming: "All watches. Summon all watches. Second Mate Wayland report to Captain McCausland. Diggers have broken through into a cavern. Seven men have fallen. All watches."

Two or three men were standing at the edge of the air-lock, gazing down the spiral staircase that wound its way into the digging.

"Who's down there?" asked Paulette.

The man saluted. "First Mate Longworth," he replied. "Six men with him. We're trying communication by radio, but haven't got in touch with him yet."

An icy hand gripped tightly at Paulette's heart.

"Adam!" she cried and was surprised to discover there were tears in her eyes, as a touch fell on her shoulder, and she looked around to see the face of Captain Walter McCausland.

"What's the matter, my dear?" he asked.

"Your dear!" she half shrieked. "I'm not your dear, and I wouldn't marry

34

you if you were the last man on Earth! You did this!"

The captain's mouth curled in a sneer. "So that's it, is it? He's persuaded you he can run you as well as the expedition. Well, I hope he can run things down where he is as well as he can everything else." He turned on his heel and walked away without another word.

*

It seemed useless to go any deeper, but Adam, driving the digging machines hard at the bottom of the excavation, was determined not to give up till he was called back. There would be no more excavations; there was no more fuel to take the *Goddard* to another spot. The lights, led down from the ship, flared about them, the tongues of the atomic power rasps worked against the rocks with an annoying, grating sound, discharging their take of powdered rock into the machine that fused it, and worked slowly around the circular wall of the excavation behind them, plastering it with white-hot material that cooled rapidly into the smooth, stony cylinder that towered far above to join with the ship.

Suddenly, one of the diggers took on a new, high-pitched note. Adam turned; and as he turned felt himself slipping, clutched at something, and the next minute was sliding down, down, a long slant it seemed into total darkness. A weight gripped him around the chest; he rolled over, but his hands caught only loose stones, and when the slide came to a stop as abrupt as its beginning, he found himself lying on his back, the weight across his legs, looking up, far up toward where a speck of light from the ship seemed miles away.

He reached out one hand and touched something as smooth as though it were polished and gently warm. "Mr. Adam!" said a voice suddenly, and he recognized it as Jake's. "Are you all right, Mr. Adam?"

"I think so, but my legs are caught."

"I'll get you free in a minute. Anybody else?"

"I got hit in the belly," came a voice. "Where's Flack?"

The engineer was lifting something. "Can you get out there now, Mr. Adam? We'll be all right in a minute." Adam gave a heave, felt his entangled legs slide free and pulled himself onto a pile of debris just as a light glared on like a star from one of the other men.

"Are we all here? Where's Flack?" There was a counting of noses and a general feeling of bodies for bruises. Above them, where the wall of the cylinder stopped, they could make out that the sudden break through had carried them down some twenty feet. "Here he is. Just an arm sticking out. I'm afraid he's done for. Come here, everyone."

One of the digging machines was brought into play and they labored to get the prisoned man free, but as they cleared the broken stone and rubble from around his face, it became evident that the effort was useless. The eyes were glazed, the head hung limp. Adam stepped back against the wall of the cave-in around them, and as he did so his hand touched it. Once more he noticed it was both smooth and warm. He turned, and in the light of the atomic lamps now blazing across the top of the cave-in examined it. It was not only smooth and warm, but polished; and just over his head he could see where the rock stopped and metal began—a clean-fitted job, a manufactured wall!

"Jake!" he called excitedly, "bring that digging machine over here for a second. The one with the cutting head."

The little engineer turned, and bounded over in a couple of steps, digging machine in hand. "Why, that's a metal wall," he cried, and applied the head for a moment in a brief surge of power. The bit cut out an inch-deep circle of metal, dropping it on some of the rubble with a tinny clang. Jake bent to pick it up.

"It's light enough to be beryllium," he said, handing the disc to Adam, and turning back to the wall, drove his cutter into it with renewed energy.

"What are you doing?" demanded the mate, hefting the disc of metal.

"This wall sounds hollow. Here goes!" He had driven the machine deep in, and stepping back, pulled the handle marked "Split." There was a sudden rending clang; a crash and a six-foot section of the wall fell inwards. The two men stared into the hole it had left, heedless of the fact that the other members of the excavating crew were crowding up behind them.

They were looking into a low square room, perhaps twenty feet across. At the far side was a doorway, and in the doorway stood a man!

To be sure he was such a man as none of them had ever before seen. He was not over four and a half feet tall, yet with arms as long as an earthling's hanging down below his knees, tremendously broad shoulders, and a head that seemed permanently pushed forward and downward above them. Below that head the creature was wrapped from neck to toe in some shimmering blue material with a metallic luster, banded around the arms and legs with red metal.

As they gazed in astonishment, the man took two steps forward, his head bobbing on his neck at each step, opened his lips, and uttered "Wahwahroo!" in a voice thick with gutturals.

*

Adam glanced around at his own men, then once more at the Plutonian dwarf, whose face, as far as he could judge, bore an expression of intense interest rather than of fear or anger. The remark, he judged, would be a greeting.

"Wahwahroo!" he replied amiably, but the Plutonian continued to stare in a manner that indicated Adam's first lesson in this unknown tongue was far from a success.

"Stand by," he remarked to the crew. "I'm going in and try to talk to this bird. May be trouble." Catching the sides of the split in the wall, he jumped down in a small cascade of pebbles that rang on the floor below in a manner which assured him this also was metal.

"I don't understand what you're saying, old man," he remarked to the Plutonian, who had remained standing in the doorway, and touching a finger to lips and ears to emphasize the point. "I don't understand, but maybe you'll be able to get it from a picture."

From one of his pockets he produced a piece of paper, and with one of the new print-pencils that had just been developed, sketched rapidly at a crude drawing of a rocket-ship with little men issuing from beneath it into the waves of an ocean.

The Plutonian accepted it from his hand, looked at it with a puzzled expression, then returned it, nodding violently, but with an expression on his face that bespoke complete lack of comprehension.

"Mr. Adam!" It was Jake's voice from the door. "I'm sending the others back with Flack to get some weapons."

"All right. Just stay there to keep up communication, Jake," Adam called back. "I'm trying to get over the idea to this guy that we're civilized."

He stepped over to the wall of the room and with his print-pencil tapped on the metal "Ping!" then twice "Ping-Ping" and then three times, "Ping-Ping-Ping."

The Plutonian watched him attentively, grimaced with thick lips, and then catching Adam's eye, tapped with his foot, once, then twice, then three times in quick succession. Adam smiled approval; the Plutonian reached out, took the drawing again and studied it gravely for a moment, then pointed at one of the little figures, at Adam, and smiled.

Adam did his best to signify that the Plutonian had grasped the point. The dwarf held up one hand, palm out toward Adam, then turned to the door behind him. Adam watched without moving, and a frown spread across the Plutonian's face.

"I got it, Mr. Adam," called Jake from the rent in the wall, "all the signals are different here. He holds up his hand to stop you because he wants you to come along."

It might be. Adam took an experimental step toward the Plutonian, and saw the latter's face clear. They reached the door together, and Adam noticed it did not open on hinges, but slid. The Plutonian touched some kind of lever or contact in the frame, uttered something in his deep voice, and stood waiting. Beyond the door, Adam noticed, was another room, perfectly dark, but as the Plutonian stopped speaking, there was a rustle of feet within and a file of half a dozen dwarfs emerged, each an exact duplicate of the first as nearly as Adam could judge. They formed a circle, staring at Adam and at the torn wall with Jake gazing through. Each in turn stepped forward, examined Adam from head to foot and having emitted a few expressive grunts took his place in the circle again. All seemed friendly, but after the last one had looked over Adam, one of the Plutonians produced some kind of weapon with a hammer-like head and a handle set cross-wise, and waved the earth-man back toward the tear in the wall.

Adam looked around at Jake, saw that he had one of the digging machines in his hand, and decided that retreat toward this protection was the best policy. But it was not the Plutonian's intention to dismiss him, evidently. One of them, whose metallic armbands were more numerous than the rest, stepped forward, reached for Adam's print-pencil, and when Adam added to it his piece of paper, was busy for a moment.

*

On the paper, when he handed it to the earth-man, were seven groups of dots, one in the first, two in the second, three in the third, regularly up to seven dots in the seventh group.

The dwarf pointed to himself, then to the single dot; and followed by indicating each of the other six Plutonians, in turn with one of the lines of dots.

When this effort at communication had been executed, he pointed to the single dot again, then to Adam, and finally to the wall.

"What does he want?" asked Jake. "What's he trying to get at?"

"I think I know," replied Adam. "See these numbers of dots? He's trying to tell me he's the number one man here, and he wants to talk to our number one man."

He turned to the Plutonian, saluting, and laughed to see the dwarf returning him a carbon copy of the movement.

"I'll stay here," he said to Jake. "As soon as they get that emergency ladder in position report to Captain McCausland and ask him whether he can come down. You might take along those metal samples you routed out. Ask Dr. Perkins to test them for beryllium. They're light and strong enough to be the stuff."

*

"General staff assembly in the mess room! Time one-two-four-five. General staff assembly in the mess room! Time, one-two-four-five. General—"

39

EXPEDITION TO PLUTO

The ship's loudspeakers were carrying the message all through the big hull, and even down into the base of the tunnel where the spiral stair of alloy had now been carried to the spot of the cave-in, and Second Mate Wayland was superintending the job of fusing some of the debris into place to strengthen and lengthen the cylinder.

Coming down the corridor toward the mess room, Adam almost ran into Paulette. She took his hand impulsively. "I'm so glad for you, Adam," she said. "You wanted this expedition to succeed so much, and you've worked so hard on it."

He smiled wryly. "Lot of good it'll do me now. The captain's going to turn in an unfavorable report and he's even now threatening to demote me to the engine room."

The girl's eyes flashed. "Never mind. You forget that I'm the power of the press. When Paulette de Vries, the radio gal, lets go, Captain Walter McCausland is going to be good and sorry for some of the things he's done."

Adam stopped and stared at her in amazement. "Why, I thought you were going to marry him!"

"Him! I wouldn't marry him if he were the last man on—on Pluto." She gave a laugh that was half a sob.

"Then—then, there's a chance—"

"Sssh. Here we are."

The scientific staff, Dr. Perkins, Professor Reuter, three assistants, the medical staff and a geographer, were at the front of the room, with the second and third mates, and the other officers of the expedition, Captain McCausland in their midst. As Adam and Paulette, the last to enter, came in, McCausland glanced at them sharply under lowered brows. Adam realized suddenly that he was holding the girl's hand and dropped it; someone laughed, and McCausland's hard, thin face was etched in a sneer.

"Miss de Vries," he said. "I called the entire staff together to listen to this report on the sample of metal brought from below, because it is very important. Would you be good enough to open your key and make a record of this report?"

40

The girl obediently snapped the switch on the device that hung at her chest, and spoke briefly into it. "Hello, Earth! Paulette speaking. We are about to hear the report on the metal found in the digging on Pluto. Dr. Perkins, our chemist, will speak first...."

Perkins' report was brief. "I have made spectroscopic tests on the metal brought from the digging, and which is used by the inhabitants of the interior of Pluto. It registers as certainly beryllium."

*

Paulette was about to speak again, when McCausland held up his hand. "I would like to hear from Professor Reuter," he said. "He conducted the chemical and physical analyses of the metal after Dr. Perkins had finished his spectroscopic tests."

Professor Reuter's oily voice boomed out. "I regret to say that although this metal responds to the spectroscopic tests for beryllium, it will not do for our purpose. It is, in fact, an isotope of beryllium, a metal which resembles it spectroscopically but not physically. The weight is wrong; the metal is much too heavy and will not do for making armor for space ships."

"But—but—" babbled Adam. "I didn't weigh it, of course, but it seemed very light to me."

"And to me also," remarked Dr. Perkins. There was a frown of puzzlement if not of suspicion between his brows.

"Miss de Vries, you will not make a record of this useless argument," snapped McCausland. "Professor Reuter will explain—"

"I will explain that the sample in its original form was full of air particles, like a fine sponge," remarked the professor easily, but with his mouth working. "The Plutonians evidently have some process of lightening in this fashion."

"Isn't there any way of treating it?"

McCausland turned to Dr. Perkins. "Will you explain to our young but over-enthusiastic friend about that?"

Dr. Perkins shook his head. The frown still persisted. "Not if it's a true isotope. That would be the same thing as transmuting elements. But I still confess I do not entirely understand."

McCausland took up the word swiftly. "Meanwhile, since it is certain that the metal used by these Plutonians will not do for our purpose, I think it important that we at least look into the composition of their civilization to some extent," he remarked. "I propose to investigate them with Professor Reuter's co-operation. Mister Longworth, you will take charge of the ship guard."

Paulette spoke up suddenly. "Captain McCausland, I think it is important that I go with you on making this contact with the Plutonians. Certainly everyone on the three planets will want to know about them."

The captain's mouth writhed a moment, and Adam noticed the glance he shot at Professor Reuter, but his voice was smooth. "To be sure, Miss de Vries. I think, then, this is all that comes before the present meeting. Dismiss."

*

The space in front of the metal wall that shut off the Plutonian domain had been cleared. As Paulette, accompanied by Professor Reuter, McCausland, and Bjornsen of the engine-room staff, reached the bottom of the dig and stepped over to it, they noted that although the wall still showed part of the jagged break, a door had been fitted to fill most of the gap.

The four stepped over to it, and McCausland tapped at the door. There was no answer at first, then from the other side there came an answering tapping—one tap, then two, then three, as though for a signal. McCausland answered in the same fashion, and after a moment the door slid back, revealing one of the strange ape men of Pluto. He saluted in a strange copy of the movement Adam had made at the time of their first contact, and McCausland, returning the salute, stepped through the door, and producing a piece of paper from his pocket began to make sketches, while the dwarf watched with interest, his face working rapidly to indicate comprehension.

After a moment the captain beckoned to Reuter and both stepped down into the Plutonian room, leaving Paulette and Bjornsen on the heap of rubble at the base of the digging. The girl looked round, then in a low voice, said to the engineer:

"Will you do me a favor?"

"Sure. What is it?"

"I'd like a souvenir. See where that part of the wall is torn? Could you break me off a little sliver of that metal to take back with me?"

"Simple." The giant mechanic stepped over to the wall and twisted at a rag of metal. It tore loose with a little ping! The other two were absorbed in their pencil-and-paper conversation with the Plutonian and did not appear to notice as Paulette slipped the fragment into the pocket of her skirt.

Bjornsen's eye looked along the crack and the fitting of the door, and he was shaking his head, clucking despondently. "These people," he said. "They are bad mechanics. Look at that joint. I'll fix it for them."

He bent and picked up one of the atomic power drills that had been left at the foot of the dig, and applying it to the wall, turned on the power. As he did so, there was a commotion; a dozen or more of the Plutonians, all dressed in the same wrappings, but with varying numbers of metal bands, came pouring through the back door of the room. McCausland turned fiercely. "Drop that!" he shouted. "Do you want to bring them all down on us?"

"I was just repairing this break for them," replied the engineer.

"Don't touch anything that doesn't belong to you," replied the captain, and turning, began to draw rapidly on his paper.

*

The crowding Plutonians, gabbling in their guttural language, were examining the work that Bjornsen had done, gazing at him admiringly and then at the power drill he had used. Three or four of them attached themselves to him, while another picked up the machine, and pulled him along as though to lead him through the rear door of the room, while their chief made a rapid drawing for McCausland.

"They want you to go with them and work for them," explained Reuter, peering over the Plutonian's shoulder as he sketched. "Just disengage their hands, gently, Bjornsen. We'll explain."

43

"Yes," said McCausland, "and go back up to the ship. You and Miss de Vries both. I don't care how important this is for purposes of record. That's an order. Go!"

Adam was on duty at the head of the spiral stair when they arrived. "Did you get it?" he asked.

Paulette put a finger on her lips and glanced at Bjornsen, then as though referring to some previous arrangement, said easily, "Do you suppose Dr. Perkins will explain the matter now?"

"I think so," he replied, catching on quickly. "I'll leave Burchall in charge of the watch and we can go up and see him at all events."

A few moments later they had reached the top of the ship where the scientific laboratories were located in a series of outer compartments. Dr. Perkins looked up from his desk as the pair entered.

"Hello, Miss de Vries," he said. "Glad to see you, Longworth. What's on your mind?"

Adam spoke. "I just wanted to ask you two questions."

"Go ahead."

"Well, the first is—what did you think of that isotope business?"

The chemist's face gathered in a frown.

"I think it was rather a tragedy. After so much effort and such high hopes! The world can go back to barbarism again now, and it will be barbarism, too. All the machinery will have to be built to use crude electric power, the standard of living will have to be reduced, and only a few people will profit—the people who own the electric plants...." He glanced at Paulette. "Is this an interview for the press?"

"No," replied Adam slowly, "and that wasn't exactly the answer I wanted. But perhaps you'll understand from the second question. Why did Professor Reuter make the test on that beryllium instead of you? I understood you were the chemist of the expedition."

*

Perkins glanced at him sharply. "I might say that you take a good deal of interest in a good many things, young man. Captain McCausland remarked about that already. But for your information, Professor Reuter is the head of the scientific staff, and is perfectly adequate to conduct so simple an examination. You aren't insinuating he isn't capable, by any chance?"

An irritated retort rose to Adam's lips, but before he could make it Paulette laid her hand on his arm and broke in: "Mr. Longworth, of course, doesn't mean to insinuate anything, Dr. Perkins. He came with me, because as press representative I felt that we ought to be perfectly sure in a matter that so vitally affects the future of the world. There are going to be quite a number of questions asked when we return and I thought we ought to have a confirming test made by you."

A curious expression flashed across Perkins' face. "Reuter should have allowed me to make one in any case, I think," he said. "Where can I get a sample?"

"I have one here." The girl produced the fragment Bjornsen had wrenched loose for her.

"You needn't mention this to anyone till we get back to the Earth," said Dr. Perkins, sawing the sample in two. "I wouldn't want to appear insubordinate. Now, let's see, we'll leave the spectroscope test out—that was made on the other sample." He sliced off a shaving, set it on the viewing table and adjusted the light. "That's odd," he remarked after a moment. "There's no sign of the air bubbles Reuter found in the other sample."

One of the other fragments he dropped into a crucible, set the dial at 900 degrees and flicked on the little motor that would melt it by atomic power heat.

Adam watched breathlessly as the oven was opened, the little molten globe of silvery metal quenched in acid, then dropped into an open-ended pipette and the container filled with liquid.

"The difference between what that pipette held and what it should hold," explained Dr. Perkins as he adjusted a scale to weigh the liquid, which had been poured off, "will be the displacement of the sample. See—2.4 cubic centimeters. Now the weight. We read it directly by putting the displaced weight in water on one arm of the scale and the sample of metal on the other. Now, when they balance the pointer—my God! Longworth!"

There was a ghost of a smile around Adam's mouth; Paulette gripped his arm. "Yes?"

"Longworth, the specific gravity is 1.93! This is more than important, it's vital! I'm going to call in my assistant and make that test over again, spectroscope and all. This is no isotope. This is perfectly genuine beryllium. How could Reuter have made such an error!"

Adam and Paulette left the chemist feverishly ringing for his assistant.

*

"I tell you, Walter, I don't like it. We've got to get out of here." Professor Reuter's usually smooth voice had an edge of worry and his fat face was haggard.

"What's the matter, losing your nerve?" taunted Captain McCausland.

The professor slapped the table of the cabin to which they had returned from their visit to the subsoil of Pluto. "I tell you, Walter, I'm risking everything by going on. My own men are wondering about that fluorine fiasco, and Perkins was just able to swallow my analysis of the beryllium and no more. I have a scientific reputation to keep up, you want to remember; it won't do me any good to succeed if I go back with my reputation for accuracy in tatters."

"Reputation!" McCausland's voice was mocking. "Just like a school girl, afraid to be caught out with the boys. Why, you old goat, if anything went wrong now, do you suppose anyone would blame me? No, they wouldn't. I only acted on the advice of my head of science. You're in this right up to the neck, Reuter, reputation or no reputation, and now you're going to see it through—on the lines I mark out for you."

The professor's weak anger collapsed. "Now, now, Walter, don't be angry. I had no intention of falling down on you. But it seems to me that I'm taking a good deal of the risk, while you—"

"While I'm going to get all the profit, I suppose? Now, listen; you have as many shares as I have. Anyway, we can settle such details at a later date. What we've got to work out now is details. That young Longworth suspects, I'm

46

sure, and he's got the girl onto his side."

The professor's voice became smooth and unctuous again. "It was too bad about that rocket-pistol. You're sure they didn't suspect anything about that?"

"Wouldn't Longworth have mentioned it? He's just the sort of hot-headed young busybody who would burst out with the whole story. No, he lost it all right. The main thing now is to keep any of the rest of them from getting a sample of that unalloyed beryllium wall down there."

"In which you are fortunately aided by the Plutonians' interest in Bjornsen. You can give orders now that the thing isn't to be touched for fear of provoking them. They're amazingly strong, physically, by the way."

"We might—" What it was that McCausland was going to suggest they might do was never finished. The buzzer at the door sounded at that moment, and as the captain said, "Come in," the pair of conspirators looked up to see a little procession, composed of Dr. Perkins, his two assistants, Adam and Paulette coming in. The face of the chemist was alight.

"Gentlemen!" he exclaimed. "I am glad to say that our expedition is a success after all. I have found another sample of beryllium and tested it. There is no indication of isotope; the weight is correct, and it has been checked by these two gentlemen. We're saved."

There was a rasping sound from Professor Reuter's throat, but McCausland's saturnine face never altered.

"And where did this other sample come from?"

"From a different portion of the wall," replied Paulette. "I found it."

"Probably beryllium exists in both forms here," remarked the captain easily. "But in any case, I hardly see how that affects our problem. What do you propose to do?"

"Do! Load up with beryllium and head for home," cried Adam.

"Unfortunately the beryllium belongs to the Plutonians. They use it in these partitioned compartments to keep out the intensely cold ocean that surrounds their planet. I do not well see how we can deprive them of it, especially over their opposition." He gathered a sheaf of papers from his desk. "Here are the notes of a picture-conversation I have had with them. They naturally decline to part with their metal. I had the idea of taking some of this isotope beryllium back with us."

There was a moment's silence in the cabin, through which came the wheezing sound of Professor Reuter's breath, heavily indrawn.

"I know that," said Adam after a moment. "Because I have just been down to the bottom of the dig, and held a picture conversation with the Plutonians. Would you be good enough to look at these, sir? The Plutonians say that they are only anxious to have these compartments built against the entrance of the ocean. When I offered to replace any beryllium we took with walls of our stronger steel alloy, they agreed at once to give us all we wanted. We can use the steel from compartment eighteen."

"Why ... that's fine, Mister Mate." Captain McCausland seemed to be drawing his breath in with some difficulty. "I congratulate you. You may start work at once."

"Oh, my Lord!" said Reuter softly.

*

"*Hello, Earth! This is Paulette de Vries, recording for later broadcast. This, folks, is our last day on the planet Pluto—our last day by Earth time, though the Plutonians wouldn't recognize it. They seem to have no sense of time or time-telling instruments. I told you in our last record how the ship has been loaded with beryllium. We have her full now of as much of the metal as we can carry. Compartment eighteen has been cut away, and the ship neatly joined together along the line of the cut, the metal that armored the compartment has been worked over into partitions to replace the beryllium from Pluto.*

"*The entire crew has been given shore leave for this last day. Only Captain McCausland and Professor Reuter will remain aboard the ship, with your radio gal, Paulette de Vries herself. I have to work up my description of the interior of Pluto, gathered on my trip a few days ago.*

"*Just for the present I'll tell you it's a wonderful world down there—four thousand miles in the center of a planet, filled with streets and houses, plants grown by artificial chemical fertilization. Never any bad weather. The Plutonians who live here have told us in their picture language that this planet was the center of life in the solar system.*

Millions of years ago, when the sun was much larger, they sent out expeditions to the other planets, of which Earth was one. We may be descendants of theirs…. Just a moment, there's someone at my door. Signing off."

She flicked off the key and opened the door to reveal Captain Walter McCausland.

"Oh, hello," she said.

"Paulette—Miss de Vries," he said earnestly, "can you come to my cabin for a few minutes? I want to say something very important to you where we won't be interrupted."

"If it's important."

"It is." He stood aside for her to pass and they moved silently down the empty corridor to his cabin. When they were seated he looked at her seriously for a moment.

"I never asked you why you took it upon yourself to break off our engagement in so dramatic a manner."

"The reason was sufficient for me. It doesn't matter otherwise."

His lips drew back. "I suppose it has something to do with that young puppy of a mate."

"That, Captain McCausland, is none of your business."

He leaned forward. "Paulette, stop fencing with me. I'll be frank. You know that not everything has gone smoothly on this expedition. You may think you know the reason; perhaps you do. And then again, perhaps I know a lot more about it than you do. You think that the expedition is a great success so far, but I want to remind you that we're not home yet. We haven't even left Pluto and those queer people down there. I think—that is—if you really want to be certain that we will get back to Earth with our load of beryllium, it might be an extremely good idea if you reconsidered your breaking the engagement."

She spoke with acidity.

"Captain McCausland, I still wouldn't marry you if you were the last man on Earth. Anything else—"

The buzzer whirred and a voice spoke through the loudspeaker system. "Professor Reuter requests Captain McCausland's presence in the laboratory.

Professor Reuter requests—"

The captain snapped his key, said, "Coming," and then turned to Paulette. "Wait here. I haven't finished. There's something more important—" and was gone, leaving her there.

*

It was a chance for which she had long hoped. Perhaps she could discover why he seemed to be intent on wrecking his own expedition. She glanced about her noting every possible location for hidden things. There was the chart rack, full of rolled maps. Not likely. Then the bookcase, rows of neat bound volumes. There remained the desk and the safe. Methodically she examined drawer after drawer, feeling sure that nothing very important would have been left so loosely about. There was nothing—but what was this? A slip of paper on which were written four numbers and the words, "Changed 4/14/2432."

She pocketed it quickly.

Hastily she went to the safe and tried out the simple number locks—to find the handle swing instantly open! Its contents were two bundles of papers. The first consisted of ancient stock certificates. Her eye glanced at the name on one, one thousand shares of Niagara Hydro to Walter McCausland. Worthless old things... but *kept in the safe!* Then the light broke. She pieced together a dozen slight references from remembered conversations—Walter's warm liking for the ancient days of electricity and steam, his hatred of modern things. He had plotted to turn the world back four centuries; to destroy the whole system that had been built on atomic power. And, she realized as she explored the thick pile of stocks that he would be the richest man in that restored world. It was a wild dream, an insane one, yet she shuddered as she thought how nearly he had succeeded.

Idly she glanced at the other slab of paper—the drawn conversations with the Plutonians. Nothing else. But why were they also kept in the safe? She glanced hurriedly through them, frowned at one, and then gasped in sheer horror as she understood it. It was an incredible drawing of dwarf men who thrust taller humans into a tank of water, while other dwarfs bowed in a strange ritual. But the horror was for the vague thing drawn inside the tank—it was impossible, yet what mistake could there be?... She must hurry ... hurry... yet she banged the safe shut and locked it, before leaving and rushing down the corridor with the bundle of drawings hugged to her gasping breast.

*

McCausland's face was drawn with some nameless thought, but his eyes narrowed shrewdly enough when he saw the girl had left. Hastily he tried the safe and found it locked. Reuter came in and asked, "Where's the girl?"

"Gone back to her cabin, most likely."

The professor's eyes glanced idly over the floor and grew large. McCausland looked where he pointed. There between desk and safe lay a stock certificate!

Reuter was the first to recover his speech. "Left her alone here, eh? Try the safe...." But McCausland was already opening it and together they stared at the empty space where the Plutonian drawings should have been.

"Search the ship!" snapped the captain. Then, "Well, Reuter, why are you looking like that?"

"You don't think she's," he licked his lips furtively, "gone down there with the others ... trying to save them...."

Captain McCausland, gray in the face, was shouting into the loudspeaker, "Paulette! Paulette!"

"She won't answer you, if she's seen those drawings," reminded Reuter.

Cursing, he rushed down the corridor to the open lock that connected with the Plutonian world below. Far down on the bottom he glimpsed a familiar tiny figure as it vanished from sight.

"Paulette! Come back." His voice was a hoarse scream. He leaned against the side of the lock and groaned.

"Walter," Reuter arrived panting, "she's gone. We can't help it. She turned you down anyway, didn't she? Let's get the ship out of here quick."

Walter's face was ghastly pale, but he straightened his back. "Do you think I'd leave *her*! Those other fools, yes! But not my girl, you old goat. She's *mine*, I tell you."

Reuter groaned.

"But they'll get you, too ... you can't leave me alone here!"

The captain turned back, snarling. "That's right. I won't leave you. You'd start the ship and leave us all, wouldn't you! Very well; you're coming, too!"

A heavy hand dragged the screaming, protesting professor into the lockdoor and pushed him savagely down on the rungs of the ladder.

*

Adam herded the forty-six sight-seers from the *Goddard* into the room. He was a little puzzled. The Plutonians now, on the last day, not only permitted but actually suggested that the crew visit their sacred temple. He looked hastily around the ante-room, trying to keep the men in order. The half dozen scientists were everywhere, poking about into things with cries of excitement. Two strangely dressed guards began throwing open the temple door and everyone surged forward. Inside, they gazed open-mouthed. The huge room was three times as high as the usual low Plutonian ceiling, on which the earthmen frequently bumped their heads. At one end was a large gallery, ten feet off the floor, and here, tier on tier, were hundreds of the dwarfs. They rose at the moment and began reciting a sonorous chant.

In the center of the room, twenty feet square, milky blue, lit from unknown depths below, was a glass tank. Adam saw, with a gasp of horror and dread, the thing that floated in it—it was a huge Amoeba. He looked shrewdly about and noted the reverent attitude of the gallery. Could this horror be the Plutonians' deity? The Great God Amoeba? Nervous now, he glanced behind and shouted. The temple doors were closing!

"Wayland! Jake!" he cried, leaping to the doors. A dozen men turned and came on the run, but they pushed and bartered in vain on the smooth metal as the doors clanged shut.

"We're prisoners!" snapped Adam. "Anyone bring a weapon ... anything at all? Even a spanner, Bjornsen? A bomb-spear, Rossiter? Don't use it, fool, you'll kill us all! Well, we're in a hell of a fix! Our bare fists! Let's get at those dam' dwarfs on the balcony, anyway. Each fellow boost his neighbor up. Ready?"

They rushed in a mob, and though the ten-foot wall meant incredible height to the dwarf Plutonians, their front ranks drew back nervously, and the rearmost made for the exits. When they saw these earthmen climb on each other's shoulders and actually drawing themselves over into the gallery they broke in a panic and milled about the exits. Great Bjornsen was among the first and while the others turned to aid their companions, he charged roaring. But a dozen of the dwarfs, dangerous as trapped rats, threw themselves on him. Three went down with pile-driver blows, skulls cracked like egg-shells, but the giant was pulled down by sheer numbers and would have been killed on the spot had not a cry from the rear of the balcony saved him. The Plutonians were through the doors, which were held open until the engineer's assailants rushed through, whereupon they closed shut. The earthmen charged and raged against them five minutes before Adam called them back.

"Save your strength, men. This is a good place to keep together and wait. It's all we can do ... they'll have to come at us some time."

*

Minutes passed, slowly, watchfully. Nerves were tense to the breaking point. Then, on the ceiling low over their heads at the back of the gallery the familiar whining snarl of one of their own atomic drills broke out. Adam crouched, muscles ready for whatever might offer. The drill droned on and the point showed through. There was a pause and with a clang a great section of the ceiling was wrenched up and fell over on the floor above. Amid the opening framed the face of Paulette de Vries!

"Come up!" she cried softly. "Oh hurry, hurry!" and into Adam's ear she poured her story, as soon as he had crawled on Bjornsen's shoulders to her side. Adam's voice immediately broke into action, urging the men to greater speed. He lay on his stomach reaching down to aid the climbers from below. Bjornsen was the last man, and as the strain of his weight fell on Adam's muscles he saw the door of the temple open and a vast mob of Plutonian guards rush in. Bjornsen was up now and Paulette tugging at Adam to come, too, but Adam had seen something—could it be! Yes, no mistake. There were two humans, still struggling, being carried across the temple floor to the great tank. A dozen dwarfs bore the leading man to its brink and with a great heave and a shout from the mob, he fell into the milky water. "It's the captain," groaned Adam, half-lowering himself as though to attempt a rescue. But Bjornsen's great arm gripped his leg. "The dirty rat," growled that giant, "he's gettin' what he planned for us. Anyway, it's hopeless, sir."

And as he dragged Adam away from the hole in the ceiling, he caught one last glimpse of Walter McCausland, frantic staring eyes pressed to the glass under water, as the great white Amoeba closed its flesh around him and the man's form became cloudy and, after a moment, ceased struggling.

"Oh Adam, hurry!" moaned Paulette.

They were in a low space, which extended in all directions, supported by squat pillars. "It's a sort of bulk-head space above their hollow world—separates them from the water above," explained the girl. "I broke into it from the dig-tunnel and if we hurry...."

"Mr. Longworth, sir," a member of the crew broke in excitedly. "I've still got this bomb-spear. I can set it and time it to go off. Why not leave it here behind us, and blow this damn bulk-head to pieces. Wipe out that lousy nest of murderers." He gripped the missile in his hands, and bent over to place it against the bulk-head wall. Adam turned to him flashingly. "None of that, Rossiter. These people are only protecting themselves. And if we flood their world, we can never come back to it for more beryllium. Come along, we've got to move.... Did you hear me, Rossiter? I said to pick up that bomb and come along."

Rossiter looked at Adam with red, fury-filled eyes. "To hell with what you said," he screamed. "These lousy freaks killed Captain McCausland. They're not going to kill me! Do you hear? They're not going to kill me! I'll blow them all to hell first. Yes, and us, too. Let me go! They'll kill me, you fool! Let me go! Ah—a-a-a-ah!" He collapsed inertly to the floor of the tunnel.

Adam sucked his bruised knuckles, his eyes like bits of flint. His gaze stabbed at the silent circle of men around him. "Anyone else feel the same way?" he asked quietly. "No? All right, we'll go on. Petersen, pick him up and carry him along. He'll be all right. He cracked, poor devil."

They raced along the bulk-head, crouching in the confined space. After what seemed ages, Paulette gasped. "Just ahead of us ... see it ... there!"

The jagged hole in the wall appeared before them, but even as they tore madly toward it, it filled with a horde of seamed, wrinkled faces, and squat, ugly bodies. Adam knew there could be no hesitating. If they stopped now, they were lost. "Don't stop," he shouted. "Keep going. Right through 'em!" With a thudding shock the earthmen met the dwarfs. Bare fists rose and fell, flailing like sledge-hammers. The brown horde fell back before the onslaught. Countless numbers were down, skulls crushed like egg shells. Then suddenly the crunch of Bjornsen's fists cleared a gap, and the desperate crew plunged into it. Ahead of them was the dig-tunnel, with its ladder leading upward to the precious safety of the space-ship. The way was clear, for the astounded Plutonians had not had time to rally their scattered forces.

But Adam knew it would not be long before they did. Across the intervening space the little party dashed, straight for the opening of the dig-tunnel. Fifty feet. Just fifty feet above them was safety. But climbing the ladder with an unconscious man among them was torturingly slow work. Adam was the last to go up. As he passed the quarter mark, he heard the enraged shouts of the dwarfs behind him. He risked one quick look over his shoulder. They were already pouring into the tunnel, and the first ranks had started to swarm the ladder. "Hurry," he gasped. "They're coming up!" Like a snail he climbed. Rung by slow rung. Time stood still. There was no sound except the panting of the earthmen above, and the ever-nearing swish of small slippered feet below. Then Adam saw that the first of his crew had reached the ship, and were clambering through the port. He saw Paulette enter, and hands reached down to help Petersen and his unconscious burden. They could go up faster now. Another moment or two and they would be safe. Adam gasped in relief as he saw the open port close above him. Three more rungs. Two! One!

Something gripped his foot. Something that pulled, and clung like a vise in spite of his frantic kicking. He looked down. Two of the Plutonians had grabbed him, and bracing themselves were pulling frantically. Helplessly he watched while long, powerful arms went out, closed about his other foot. He felt it pulled from the rung, and now he hung there, held only by his arms that grasped the rung above him. Arms that creaked in their sockets, until darting streaks of pain shot across his eyes. Hands that were wet with sweat, slipping ... slipping....

"Quick sir. Here!" Adam's staring eyes saw the huge figure of Bjornsen leaning from the port above him. But so far above him. The man could never reach him. Then he felt strong huge hands that gripped him by the arm-pits and pulled. Pulled until he thought his body must tear in two. But he was going up! With the last of his strength he kicked his feet viciously, trying to dislodge those straining, sinewy hands that gripped his legs. Then suddenly, they let go. Like a limp bag of sand he was hauled through the port, and lay gasping on the flooring. "Quick!" he croaked. "The door. Close it." With the clang of metal against metal he heard it shut, and lay back, drawing in great lungfuls of cool, refreshing air. After a moment he clambered rockily to his feet. His eyes met those of Bjornsen. His hand went out, and was clasped in the Norwegian's great paw. "Thanks," he said quietly. "I shall never forget that." He shook his head, and passed an aching arm across his eyes. Some measure of strength returned to him, and with it the realization that as officer in command, there was much to be done. "To your stations, men. Prepare to ascend immediately. Close the inner hatch. We're not safe yet. They have our atomic drills, and if they start to use them on the ship, we're lost. Mr. Wayland, come with me. Jake, to your engines."

With Paulette at their heels, Adam and Wayland hurried along the passages of the great ship until they reached the control room. "Engines ready, Jake?" he asked into the radiophone. "Stand by. Very well, Mr. Wayland. Six ascensions please."

Wayland gasped. "Six, sir! Why that'll tear the ship to pieces. She won't stand it, sir!"

Adam fixed him with cool eyes. "I said six ascensions, Mr. Wayland."

Wayland opened his mouth to protest further, then closed it with a snap.

"Very good, sir. Six ascensions, sir." He seized a lever to the left of the control board, moved it to neutral, then shoved it hard over. Six red lights glowed suddenly on the board. For a moment nothing happened, then deep in the bowels of the great ship a low, almost inaudible whine started. Like a siren it rose in pitch and tone, until it sounded like a hundred banshees screaming and wailing. A great shudder passed through the ship from stem to stern. Like a wounded beast struggling to rise she strained upward from the bottom of the icy ocean until it seemed she must tear herself to flying, screaming fragments. Wayland's eyes were filled with fear. Paulette stared unblinkingly, breathless, at Adam. Little beads of sweat stole out on his forehead, but with a calm he didn't feel he forced himself to keep his eyes on the panel before him. "Let me know the moment we're clear," he ordered. For a long minute no one spoke. Then from the control board a voice: "We're clear, sir."

Wayland's eyes lost their wild look. A great sigh heaved from his lips, and he slumped to trembling relaxation. Paulette uttered a single, glad cry, then sank gently to the floor, while great sobs racked her bowed head and trembling shoulders. "Reduce to two ascensions, Mr. Wayland." Adam's voice was hoarsely unsteady. "In two minutes plot your course and shift your engines. We're heading home." Then in two steps he was beside Paulette, was bending over to pick up the sobbing girl. He held her close, with her arms curved tightly around his neck, and her head buried in his broad shoulder.

*

It was a quiet group that gathered some two hours later in the main cabin of the *Goddard*. Every member of the crew was there. Deep within the great hull the engines were running smoothly. Outside the glassed ports the dark blue heavens stretched away on all sides. Like the shimmer of a thousand diamonds against a velvet backdrop the suns of the Milky Way danced and glowed. At Adam's side sat Wayland and Paulette. Adam looked at those before him. "At ease, gentlemen. With the grace of good fortune we are on our way home. The expedition is a success. A success, that is, materially. As you all know, we have lost Captain McCausland and Dr. Reuter. If I am correct, you all know also the reason, and the manner in which we lost them.

Perhaps Captain McCausland is not entirely to blame. Perhaps it is given to every great man to fail once. Whatever the reason, he has always been—up to this trip—a hero to all of us, and to the world. I must of course make a complete report of his death. That report will be: 'Killed by the Plutonians in defense of his ship and his crew.'"

For a long moment no one spoke. Then Paulette, with tears of happiness dimming her eyes, turned and gripped Adam's hand in her own. "My dear," she smiled, "thank you." As Adam turned to her, he felt Wayland gripping his other hand tightly. "I understand, sir. Nothing will be said." Adam smiled tenderly at Paulette, then his eyes turned anxiously to search those of his crew. On every face was a commending grin of approval. In every pair of eyes was a promise that had been given, and would be kept. With a suspicious huskiness in his voice, Adam drew himself erect. "Thank you gentlemen," he said softly. The crew filed out.

With his arm around Paulette, he drew her gently to the starboard port, and pointed to a dim, fast-receding, silver-green orb. "There it is, darling. I don't know whether to curse it or bless it." He grinned at her quizzically. She came close to him, and her arms stole gently about him. "I'll bless it as long as I live," she breathed.

He held her close. His head bowed to meet her soft, red lips.

"Beg pardon, sir." Wayland's voice sounded far away.

"Yes?" Adam did not turn his head.

"The course it set, sir. Any further orders, sir?"

"Yes, Mr. Wayland. One."

"Yes, sir?"

"Get out, Mr. Wayland."

Lightning Source UK Ltd.
Milton Keynes UK
UKHW011950230720
367075UK00007B/312